FOLLOW THE TRACK

ALL THE WAY BACK

To Edward, with love ~T.K.

For Maisie Mantle ~B.M.

First published 2017 by Walker Books Ltd
87 Vauxhall Walk, London SE11 5HJ

2 4 6 8 10 9 7 5 3 1

Text © 2017 Timothy Knapman
Illustrations © 2017 Ben Mantle

The right of Timothy Knapman and Ben Mantle to be identified
as author and illustrator respectively of this work has been asserted by them
in accordance with the Copyright, Designs and Patents Act 1988

This book has been typeset in New Century Schoolbook

Printed in China

British Library Cataloguing in Publication Data:
a catalogue record for this book is available from the British Library

ISBN 978-1-4063-6059-2

www.walker.co.uk

FOLLOW THE TRACK

ALL THE WAY BACK

Timothy Knapman

illustrated by Ben Mantle

WALKER BOOKS
AND SUBSIDIARIES

LONDON • BOSTON • SYDNEY • AUCKLAND

Today was a BIG day
for Little Train.
He was going out on the track,
all by himself,
for the very first time!

Little Train felt nervous.

He *chugga-chugged* forward very carefully.

Then he *chugga-chugged* back very carefully.

The track felt slip-slidey under his wheels.

Hmm.

He wasn't so sure.

"Don't worry," said Mummy Train.

"You can do it," said Daddy Train.

So Little Train took a deep breath –

"CHOOOOO!" –

and he *chugga-chugged* along
the track a little more.

Slowly at first.
Then a bit faster.

"Remember, when it's time to come home,"
   said Mummy Train.
"No matter how far away you are,"
   said Daddy Train.
"Just follow the track all the way back,"
   said Mummy and Daddy Train together,
"where we'll be waiting for you."

But Little Train was going really fast now,
and he hadn't been listening properly.

"YIPPEEE!" he whistled, as he
went chugging out into the world.

The first thing he saw was a great green field.

"WOO-WOO!"

It was so wide!

"CLICKETY-CLACK, CLICKETY-CLACK!"

sang Little Train,
as he went running through the field.
And when he got to the end,
the track led him on...

Over a bridge.
It was so high!
He could see
all around him
for miles and miles.

"RATTLY-TAT, RATTLY-TAT!"

sang Little Train,
as he went rattling across
the bridge.

And when he got to the other
side, the track led him on...

Up the side of a mountain.
It was so steep!
Little Train had never
been up so high before.

**"CLUMPETY-CLIP,
CLUMPETY-CLIP,
CLUMPETY-CLIP!"**

sang Little Train,
as he went climbing up
the mountain.

And when he got to the top,
the track led him on...

To a roaring, rolling river.
The water was rushing
and splushing so fast!

"ZIPPETY-ZOOM, ZIPPETY-ZOOM!"

sang Little Train,

as he went racing by the river.

But when the river reached the sea...

There was no track left.

Little Train shivered.
He'd come such a long way –

through a field,
across a bridge,
up a mountain,
along a river –

and no matter how hard
Little Train looked,
he couldn't see the warm,
bright lights of home.

He was all alone at the edge of the world,
and it was getting dark.

He missed his Mummy and Daddy Train.

What was he going to do?

And then ...
he remembered.

"When it's time to come home,"
said Mummy Train, "no matter
how far away you are..."

"OF COURSE!" cried Little Train.
So he took a deep breath,
and he *chugga-chugged* back –

"CHOOOOO!" –

to where the track curved around
so he was facing the right way.

"WOO-WOO!"

And he followed the track...

"ZIPPETY-ZOOM!"   **"CLUMPETY-CLIP!"**

along the river,   up the mountain,

"RATTLY-TAT!"
across the bridge,

"CLICKETY-CLACK!"
through the field.

And all the way back …

HOME
where his Mummy and Daddy
were waiting for him.

"LITTLE TRAIN!" they said.

And the very next day, Little Train was out on the slip-slidey track again, all by himself ...

in search of even BIGGER adventures!